# Yonie Wondernose

# Yonie Wondernose

## by

## Marguerite de Angeli

DOUBLEDAY

NEW YORK  LONDON  TORONTO  SYDNEY  AUCKLAND

To place a credit card order of $25.00 or more, call toll free 1-800-223-6834 EXT. 9479. In New York, please call 1-212-492-9479. Or send your order plus $2.00 shipping and handling to the following address: Doubleday Readers Service, Dept. MD, P.O. Box 5071, Des Plaines, IL. 60017-5071. Prices and availability are subject to change without notice. Please allow four to six weeks for delivery.

*Published by Doubleday, a division of Bantam Doubleday Dell Publishing Group, Inc.*
*666 Fifth Avenue, New York, New York 10103*

*Doubleday and the portrayal of an anchor with a dolphin are trademarks of Doubleday, a division of Bantam Doubleday Dell Publishing Group, Inc.*

*Library of Congress Cataloging-in-Publication Data*
*De Angeli, Marguerite, 1889–1987*
*Yonie Wondernose / by Marguerite de Angeli.*
*p. cm.*
*Summary: A curious Amish boy who lives on a Pennsylvania Dutch farm shares a wonderful secret with his father.*
*[1. Farm life—Fiction.   2. Amish—Fiction.   3. Pennsylvania Dutch—Fiction.]   I. Title.*
*PZ7.D35Yo 1989*
*[Fic]—dc19        88-38827*
*CIP*
*AC*
*ISBN 0-385-07573-1*

for
Three Little Wondernoses ❀❀❀

Nina   David
and
Kiki

# Introduction

*Yonie Wondernose* was a continuation of Mama's fascination with, and admiration of the Amish, a community of "Plain" People living in Lancaster County, Pennsylvania.

She often held them up to us children as examples of how to behave, or get along without the latest modern conveniences, and still be happy.

As in most of her books, it contains gentle lessons for young readers and still entertains, while demonstrating the importance of family relationships.

Mama spent quite a lot of time in and around Lancaster, and lived with two families there for a few days on several occasions. As usual, her hosts "adopted" her after she spent a day or two in their company.

Harry E. de Angeli

*January 1989*

Yonie was a little Pennsylvania Dutch boy. He was seven. He lived with Mom and Pop, Malinda, Lydia, and little Nancy on a farm in Lancaster County. His brother Ammon was grown up and had been away for a long time. Granny lived on the farm, too. She lived in her own part of the house. But most of the time she was in the kitchen helping Mom and Malinda.

Yonie's real name was Jonathan, but everyone called him Yonie. Pop called him "Yonie Wondernose" because he was so curious. He wanted to know about everything. If Pop brought a package into the house, he must see what was in it. If the Bishop came to talk to Pop, he must listen. If Mom had a pot boiling on the stove, he must lift the lid to see what was cooking. Sometimes the steam burned his nose, but it didn't keep him from looking the next time. If Malinda was baking a cake, Yonie was sure to open the oven door to see what kind it was.

"A Wondernose you are for sure!" she would scold. "Look now how it falls so fast!"

When Yonie and Lydia were on their way to school, he stopped so many times that they were often late. He hung over the fence to watch the men filling the wagons with stones from the stone crusher. He stood watching while a man changed a tire on a car, or while Nathan Straub seeded the bean field.

"We'll be late!" wailed Lydia. "Come now!" But she stood to watch, too!

Yonie's jacket was fastened with hooks and eyes instead of buttons. Pop didn't have buttons on his suit either. That is because he was an Amishman. And the Amish people never use buttons unless they are necessary. Yonie wore a broad hat just like Pop's hat, too—a straw one in summer and a black felt one in winter. And Mom cut Yonie's hair around a bowl, just like she cut Pop's. But Pop wore a beard such as all Amishmen wear.

This afternoon Pop and Mom were going visiting. They were taking Malinda and Lydia with them in the Germantown wagon, and they would stay overnight. Granny, Yonie, and Nancy stood in the doorway to see them off.

"Good-by," said Pop. "Don't be a Wondernose, now, and forget what you are doing!"

"No, Pop, I won't," Yonie answered.

"Remember, you are the man of the house now," said Mom.

"Ya, I will." Yonie nodded and stood straighter.

"Take good care of the barn creatures," called Pop again. "Feed and water them well. Don't forget, if anything happens, be sure to look after the horses first. They get scared so fast. Next, look after Dunder the red bull. He cost a lot of money, so take good care of him, don't forget! We see, now, if you are a man!"

Then he winked, and Yonie knew what he meant. Pop had promised him something when he was old enough to be trusted like a man, but no one, not even Mom, knew about that promise. It was a secret between Pop and Yonie.

"I won't forget!" he called back.

As the wagon drove off, he thought, "Now Pop thinks I'll be a Wondernose, but I'll show him! I'll show him how big and smart I can be! When he comes home tomorrow, he'll see that I can take care of the animals by myself. Then, maybe, he'll let me do what he promised!"

"*Ya,* vell," said Granny. "Soon it makes time for supper. More rountwood I need for the fire, and the cistern water iss all! The last I used for sprinkling the plants and for scrubbing."

Cistern water was soft rainwater that Granny liked best for washing dishes and such things. Pop teased Granny because she was always scrubbing.

"It's a wonder you don't scrub the hoe handles and the fence posts, you are so clean!" he would say.

But Granny only said, "Better so, as like some I know, with floors all smeary and things all hoodled up!" and went on scrubbing. Yonie knew he must pump a lot of water to keep Granny supplied. He must get the wood for the kitchen stove. But he must take care of the animals, too.

He went first to the pasture for the cows, Blossom, Bluebell, and Buttercup. As they ambled down the lane, a squirrel scolded at Yonie from the fence rail, then scampered up a tree and into a knothole. Yonie *must* see where he went. Up the tree he scrambled and peered into the hole.

He thrust his finger in to see what he could find. But he drew it out again in a hurry, for Mr. Squirrel gave it a sharp bite!

"Ach!" Yonie scolded himself, "here I am, being a Wondernose, just like always."

When he climbed down from the tree, the cows had scattered to nibble the grass at the edges of the lane. It took Yonie some time to get them started again in the right direction and to their places in the cow shed. He hurried to throw down fresh straw for their beds, while Granny milked. He carried water for them and called Nancy to come and put milk in the cats' dish for Malta and the four kittens.

He took the horses to the trough for water. He patted Star's broad back and thought of what Pop had promised. Then he went to look after Dunder. Dunder was kept in a pen and shed of his own on the far side of the barn.

Yonie had helped Pop, but he had never taken care of Dunder by himself as Ammon always had. He knew he must speak quietly to the great beast. He knew how to use the staff that Pop kept handy, too, and how to attach it to the ring in the bull's nose. So he felt safe, even though Dunder was so big and fierce.

The summer was really over. The hay was in the barn and the harvest gathered. But it had turned very warm again. Yonie's shirt was damp from the heat, and his yellow hair clung to his forehead. He wished he could stop work and go wading in the creek. The Little Conestoga ran through the meadow, and Yonie knew how cool it would be in the shade of the willow tree on its bank. He dropped the bucket he was carrying and started toward the creek. Then he remembered his promise to Pop—and Pop's promise to him. He picked up the bucket and went to pump more water for the rest of the animals and the chickens.

"Ach, vell," he told himself, "I can douse good, once, when I get the chores done."

He grunted as he lifted the heavy pail out of the trough. The water spilled a little onto his bare feet. It felt good and made clean patterns where it washed off the dust. He carried the bucket as full as he could. The chicken pans had to be filled, the calves needed a drink, the pigs had to be fed, and there was still the water to carry in for Granny.

When Yonie had filled the pans in the chicken yard, he made sure to lock the chicken house door. He knew the eggs had been gathered, so he didn't bother to look inside again.

He picked up the buckets in a hurry to water the calves and then stopped. Was that an airplane he heard? He couldn't see it, but now he remembered that Granny wanted the roundwood for the fire.

"Rountwood gives a hot fire," she had said, "and supper makes soon."

So Yonie went to the woodpile to get it. He could see Nancy under the big tree happily playing with her doll.

He started to gather the wood, and again came the deep purr of an airplane. This time he was sure. It might even be a new kind. He dropped the wood and ran to the corner of the house where he could see better.

As he craned his neck to follow the flight of the plane, he heard Nancy call, "Wonderno-ose Yonie! Wonderno-ose Yonie!" she teased.

He made a face in Nancy's direction, but turned back to the woodpile. When he carried the wood into the kitchen, Granny wasn't there. Something was bubbling on the stove. It smelled so good! He *must* see what was inside! Could it be apple dumplings? He lifted the lid. Ouch! The steam burned his nose, as usual.

He wondered where Granny could have gone, leaving the supper to cook by itself. But there was more work to do, so he went out to pump water for the calves. The water made him think again of the cool Conestoga. How he wished he were in it! It wouldn't take long for a splash, he thought, and it would feel so good! Suddenly he dropped the pump handle and started for the creek. He had his shirt and trousers off almost before he got there, and then—in he went.

The coolness and the quiet murmur of the creek made Yonie stay longer than he meant to. Then in the stillness he heard the bleating of the calves, and suddenly remembered that they were thirsty. He pulled on his clothes as best he could without drying and hurried back to the pump.

When he opened the barnyard gate, the calves came running to get at the water. The little black-and-white one nipped at Yonie's trousers, butted him with his knobbly head, and licked at his hands to see if he had any sugar.

Yonie thought, "That little runt now, if he was mine, I'd call him Wondernose like Pop calls me, the way he's nosing into my hand for sugar! I wish he *was* mine! It would be more fun to water them if one could be mine. If Pop would give me even a little pig the next time there are any, I'd take care of it till it grew big."

But more than he wanted the calf, more than the little pig, Yonie wanted what Pop had promised. He closed the gate and hurried to get the sour milk for the pigs. He could hear them squealing around beyond the corner of the barn.

When they saw Yonie coming with their supper, they squealed more loudly than ever. There were vegetable parings, bits of bread, and celery tops floating in it. But the pigs thought it was delicious. The great big old sow put both feet in the trough so as to be sure and get her share.

When Yonie went to the kitchen with the water for Granny, she still wasn't there. He thought, once, that he heard her call. But when he listened again he heard nothing.

The food in the kettle had boiled over and didn't smell so good as it had before. He called up the stairs, "Granny! Oh, Granny! Somesing smells like burning!" But there was no answer.

He called again, then listened. But there was still no answer. Then he went upstairs and looked in all of the rooms. But still he saw no one and heard nothing. He went downstairs and over into Granny's part of the house.

"Granny!" he shouted, but only the ticking of the clock answered him.

As he stood watching where Granny might be, his eyes lighted on the painted chest. There Granny kept the old book. It was full of stories that Yonie loved to hear. Granny never allowed the children to open the chest themselves.

She always said, "The things in it are over two hundred years old. That's when your great-great-great-grandfather came with his family and many others from the old country. They came so they might worship God in their own way."

Yonie thought, "It wonders me, now, what else is in there besides the book. I could just look once, and Granny would never know."

He went to the chest where it stood under the window and lifted the lid. But before he could even begin to see anything, he seemed to hear Pop's voice, saying, "Yonie! Yonie Wondernose!"

He stood for a second, then was sure that he heard a voice.

It sounded like a real voice coming through the open window.

He listened. He could just barely hear it. But it called, "Yonie! Oh, Yonie!"

He dropped the lid with a bang! Out he flew, through to the kitchen, to the porch, down the yard, through the arbor, and to the chicken house.

Now he could hear the voice plainly, and it was coming from inside the chicken house. "Yonie! Ach, Yonie! Let me out of here!"

He turned the lock and opened the door and out fell Granny! She

had been shut up in the heat of the chicken house ever since Yonie filled the water pans! Yonie helped her to a seat in the arbor and ran to get her a drink of water.

When she could speak, she said, "Ach, Yonie! Why didn't you be *this* time a *Wondernose*? Always look *first* inside, *then* lock the door." But Yonie looked so sorry that Granny had to laugh.

"Never mind," she said. "You locked the door like your Pop said. You didn't know Granny was in there. Next time—look inside first." She sniffed the air. "Somesing smells like burning," she said. "Supper, I guess. Ach, vell, ve have spreadin's anyways on our bread, and shoofly pie. Call Nancy."

They went in to supper.

Nancy helped Granny put the "spreadin's" on the table. There was apple butter, currant jelly, stewed apples, and piccalilli. Then there was the pie. It was a shoofly pie made with soft molasses cake baked in a piecrust. Yonie was very fond of it. While they were eating, Granny told how it felt to be shut up in the chicken house.

"Hot as seven in a bed it was in there! I counted the chickens over and over. They stare at me, and cluck like I don't belong in there. And I stare back. I try to get out by the place where the chickens go in, but for a long time now I'm too big for that!"

Yonie and Nancy laughed to think of Granny down on her hands and

knees trying to get through that little opening. Yonie thought how it would be to sleep seven in a bed!

"Whew!" he said.

Yonie wished he could douse again in the creek; it was so warm in the kitchen. Granny looked warm, too, and fanned herself with her apron. Even Nancy pushed little wisps of hair up onto her braids.

Suddenly, as they finished eating, the spot of sunlight faded from the table, and there was a growl of thunder.

"It makes like a storm, ain't, Granny?" said Yonie.

"*Ya,*" agreed Granny. "The heat iss something wonderful. It makes a storm, maybe. Make everything fast by the barn."

Nancy ran out to get her doll. And Yonie went to make sure he had done all that Pop told him to do. Yes, he had fed and watered the barn creatures. They were all quiet for the night. When he came in, it was time for him to go to bed.

There was another grumble of thunder, but Yonie didn't hear it. He was asleep.

Suddenly a bright flash woke him with a start. With the flash came a sizzling "bang" of thunder! Yonie jumped out of bed. He knew the storm had broken right overhead and that something might have caught fire from the lightning.

"Ach!" he thought. "Somesing does happen maybe, like Pop said. Now I have to see if Star and Blackie are all right and Dunder."

He reached for his breeches just as Granny came hurrying to the foot of the stairs. She called, "Yonie! Oh, Yonie! Come quick!"

But she didn't need to tell him the barn was afire. He could see it as he ran past the window and down the steep, twisty stairs. Then the rain began.

Yonie didn't wait for Granny, who was tying her shoes. He ran

headlong through the shower toward the barn. Something black flew past him, then four somethings. It was Malta and the four kittens. A cloud of pigeons fluttered about, then flew off toward the woods. They lived in the cupola of the barn.

Now a blaze came out of the barn like a great red flower that grew and grew, even though the rain was coming down faster and faster. Yonie had to hold his breath as he tried to go through the thick smoke that already filled the barn. If he was going to get the horses out, he would have to cover their heads. Otherwise, Pop had told him, they would run right back into the fire again.

Yonie knew where to find the old carriage robe that Pop kept hanging near the horses just in case of need. Stumbling toward it, he got it in his hands at last. Then he hurried to hang it over Star's head. Granny came running in with her shawl to put over Blackie and got him out of the barn door just behind Yonie and Star.

Lightning flashed and thunder banged. Rain poured down, but the fire burned fiercer and roared louder, for now it had reached the hay.

"Run!" cried Granny. "Quick now! Over past the house, and we tie the horses to the fence post."

Blackie tossed his head and tried to get away, but Granny held on. Star snorted and neighed and tried to fling off the cover from his head. But Yonie held it tight till they reach the fence. The rain stopped as suddenly as it had begun, and a breeze sprang up.

Back raced Yonie and Granny toward the barn. Granny was breathing hard.

"Run ahead and let loose the chickens!" she cried. "The wind blows that way and sparks soon set fire to the roof."

"*Ya!*" Yonie shouted, as he turned off to let out the chickens. They ran out scolding and clucking, and scattered over the road and fields.

"It's good I ain't in there still!" panted Granny. "The fire makes worse on this side, so we loose the cows next. Then Dunder."

They got Blossom and Buttercup out safely and left them to run toward the orchard. But before they could get Bluebell out of the way, a burning brand fell across her back. It rolled off, but left a scorched place. She leaped clear of the door in one jump, then ran off after the other cows.

Granny and Yonie got out just in time, and ran to open the calf pen, which was close by.

"How shall we fix poor Bluebell so the burn won't hurt?" panted Yonie.

"Apple butter," gasped Granny, spreading her skirts to head off the

calves so they would go the right way. "Apple butter makes the pain go away. I fix it while you get Dunder out. Get him quick! He's such a fine bull, your Pop gets mad if he's hurt! Quick!"

Granny started off toward the house, and Yonie hurried around to the front of the barn toward Dunder's shed. He could see the bare frame of the roof through the fire. And just as he looked up, a great timber fell.

"It must be right on the ground near the pigpen!" he thought excitedly. "I *must* see where it went. Besides, what of the pigs and the old sow?"

He turned back the way he had come and went around to where the pigs were shut in beyond the calf pen. The timber had fallen inside the barn, and not on the pigpen. But Yonie opened the door and called to them, making a sucking noise with his mouth as if he were going to feed them. They came rushing up. And Yonie guided them through the gate and down the slope to the field where Pop had been digging potatoes. There they began rooting in the ground, so Yonie knew they were safe.

Back he started across the muddy field toward Dunder's pen, for now he could hear great roars from that direction.

"That Dunder, now," he thought, "he might do me somesing, he's so mad. He bellers wonderful! If only Pop would come home!"

A sudden burst of flame made him stop to look and wonder. A great rafter fell with a shower of sparks as he watched.

"It's like a picture in a book!" he thought.

Dunder bellowed again, more loudly than ever. Yonie set his tired legs in motion. How he wished Pop were here! But Pop wasn't here, and Dunder must be gotten out!

Then, above the whooshing and the crackling of the fire, Yonie heard a new noise. He stopped again. He looked out toward the highway.

The road leading down from it was crowded with people! There were people in wagons, people in carriages, people in automobiles, and people on foot! Yonie stared. Then a siren shrieked, and he heard a bell clanging. That must be the fire engine! He started to run toward the crowd. He must see that beautiful, bright red engine that now turned into the road. It puffed and clanged. It made the horses step lively. It pushed the people off the road and sent the chickens squawking in every direction.

Yonie was so excited that he forgot everything else. He forgot about the tools and farm gear that needed to be moved from the fire. He forgot that Granny might need his help with Bluebell. He forgot Nancy, who was

still asleep in the brick house. He even forgot Dunder. All he could think of was that red engine with the shiny trim.

Just as he was about to cross the cornfield Dunder bellowed again loud and long. Yonie stopped short.

"Ach!" he thought, "that Dunder!"

He stood for a second, longing to go where the red engine was already at work. He could see the stream of water it was pouring into the fire from the Little Conestoga. He could see the fire dying down.

Then he seemed to hear Pop say, "Wondernose!"

He turned and ran as fast as he could go to Dunder's pen. Beside the gate into the pen Pop kept the long staff with the hook at the end. Yonie made sure to have it securely in hand before he opened the gate. He could tell that Dunder was not very happy.

Yonie crept up toward the big bull's head. Dunder started to roar, and Yonie quickly snapped the staff into place. Dunder tossed his head, but not far! He was stopped suddenly by the pain in his nose, for the staff thrust his head up into the air and he was helpless.

Yonie was very proud to lead him through the gate toward the field

that sloped up the hill. He wrapped Dunder's chain around the trunk of a tree and left the staff where it would be handy. But Dunder still bellowed as if he were in pain.

"Now, what makes it that you holler still?" Yonie said out loud. "Maybe you don't like all this fire, but to make so much noise is no good." He turned to go back toward the fire engine. And then he saw the cause of Dunder's bellows. Across Dunder's back where there should have been glossy brown hair there was no skin at all! A burning timber had fallen

on the big bull before Yonie had moved him. Yonie ran tearing down the hill to find Granny and the apple butter.

He had to push his way through the crowd of people. Granny was

on the back porch comforting Nancy, who stood there crying in her little nightgown.

He could see her in the light from the kitchen where neighbor women were already setting about making coffee.

"Why," thought Yonie, "it's almost like a picnic!"

He started to cross the wagon track. But just then a shiny black car drove in and stopped. Yonie forgot Dunder again. He *must* see that car! Pop said automobiles were worldly, but Yonie loved to look at them. He stood staring.

The door opened and someone got out—someone who looked like Pop! Someone who said, just like Pop, "A Wondernose still!" It *was* Pop! A neighbor had gone to bring him home!

"And are the barn creatures all safe?" asked Pop.

But before Yonie had time to answer, the Bishop and several neighboring farmers came up to tell Pop they would help him to rebuild the barn and get things in order again.

Yonie wished he could see Pop alone for just one minute, then he could explain that Dunder was hurt because he had taken care of the pigs first! What would Pop do when he knew that Yonie almost forgot Dunder because he stopped to look at the red engine?

He stood waiting till the men were through talking. Then he took a long breath and began: "Apple butter makes good for the burns on Dunder's back, Granny says. And I forgot and took the pigs out first." There! It was out!

What would Pop say? Would he say, "Now you are too little still for me to keep that promise?"

But Pop didn't say anything. He just took Yonie up in his arms and

held him tight. Then he put him down again, and said, "Now, come, we see where all the animals are. Star and Blackie I saw when we come in the lane. Where's Dunder?"

When they reached the top of the field where Dunder was tied, some of the neighbor women were there, putting a poultice on Dunder's back. Dunder was quiet.

"He's not bad hurt," said Katie Lapp. "We heard him beller as we come over the field. I bring apple butter like always when there is a fire, to put on the animals when they get hurt."

Pop thanked them. Then he and Yonie went on down to the potato field where the pigs were. They were still hunting out roots in the mud,

all but the mother sow. She lay over in the fence corner. When Yonie leaned over to see if she was all right, what do you think he saw? Ten little new baby pigs! Pop saw them, too. He laughed.

"*Ya,* vell," he said, "this time it pays to be a Wondernose! Better

Dunder gets a pain in his back as lose the old mother sow!"

Yonie felt happy.

"Now," said Pop, "for being such a big smart boy, one of these little pigs belongs to you. Choose which one."

Yonie didn't speak. He just laid his hand on the little pink one that couldn't find room to get his share of dinner. Now he had a pet that was all his own.

The calves came bleating to the other side of the fence. The little black one put his nose through the rails and sniffed in Yonie's pocket as he leaned over.

"He's a Wondernose just like you," said Pop. "Would you like to have him, too?"

"*Ya,* Pop," said Yonie. "I'd like fine to have him!"

"It takes a *man* to care for barn creatures and get them safe out of a fire. Soon it makes time for fall planting." He winked again at Yonie. "I need a man for that, too!" he said.

Now Yonie knew that Pop would keep his promise! At last he could do what he had hoped for ever since Ammon left. He was big enough now to guide the two great work horses to harrow the field for winter wheat all by himself. He could see himself astride Star's back, high above the ground, above the fence posts, even above Pop's head! He could hear himself saying, "GEE! HAW!" and whichever way he said, the horses would go! He slipped his hand into Pop's big one.

"Yonie Wondernose!" said Pop.

## About the Author

*Marguerite de Angeli* was born in 1889 in Lapeer, Michigan. During her long, productive life she wrote twenty-eight books for young readers that won her a large and faithful audience as well as many prestigious awards. The honors she received include the Newbery Medal, two Caldecott Honor Awards, the Lewis Carroll Shelf Award, and the Regina Medal. A mother, grandmother, and great-grandmother, Mrs. de Angeli found her own family a vital source of inspiration. Each of her books reflects the wisdom and personal warmth that has earned her a special place in the hearts of generations of young readers.